Oona in the Arctic

For Susi and our old-friends kind of magic. —K.D.

To Life! —R.F.

With thanks to Inuit artist and activist Holly Mititquq Nordlum, enrolled member
of the Native Village of Qikiktagruq, for her collaboration and contributions.

Katherine Tegen Books is an imprint of HarperCollins Publishers.

Oona in the Arctic
Text copyright © 2023 by Kelly DiPucchio
Illustrations copyright © 2023 by Raissa Figueroa
All rights reserved. Manufactured in Italy.
No part of this book may be used or reproduced in any manner whatsoever without written
permission except in the case of brief quotations embodied in critical articles and reviews.
For information address HarperCollins Children's Books, a division of HarperCollins Publishers,
195 Broadway, New York, NY 10007.
www.harpercollinschildrens.com

Library of Congress Cataloging-in-Publication Data
Names: DiPucchio, Kelly, author. | Figueroa, Raissa, illustrator.
Title: Oona in the Arctic / words by Kelly DiPucchio ; pictures by Raissa Figueroa.
Description: First edition. | New York, NY : Katherine Tegen Books, [2023] | Audience: Ages
4-8. | Audience: Grades K-1. | Summary: "A mermaid and her otter friend go on a journey to
help a lost beluga whale return to the Arctic"— Provided by publisher.
Identifiers: LCCN 2022000112 | ISBN 978-0-06-322232-8 (hardcover)
Subjects: CYAC: Mermaids—Fiction. | White whale—Fiction. | Whales—Fiction. |
Lost and found possessions—Fiction. |
Arctic regions—Fiction. | LCGFT: Picture books. | Fiction.
Classification: LCC PZ7.D6219 Or 2023 | DDC [E]—dc23
LC record available at https://lccn.loc.gov/2022000112

The artist used Procreate to create the digital illustrations for this book.
Typography and lettering by Molly Fehr
22 23 24 25 26 RTLO 10 9 8 7 6 5 4 3 2 1
First Edition

Oona
in the Arctic

words by
Kelly DiPucchio

pictures by
Raissa Figueroa

 KATHERINE TEGEN BOOKS
An Imprint of HarperCollins Publishers

Oona loved surprises.

Shiny pearl surprises.

Coral reef surprises.

Sandy beach surprises.

But when a baby beluga whale unexpectedly appeared one morning in the cove, Oona jumped, and her basket of shells went flying.

"How in the world did you get here?" Oona cooed at the baby. She had never seen a beluga whale in the warm waters where she lived.

The poor calf looked lost and frightened.

Otto wasted no time trying to make their new visitor feel welcome.

Oona did the same, offering her a slice of kelp cake.
And then another.
And another.

When the cake was gone, the hungry whale ate ninety-nine sushi rolls,
a bucket of chowder, and an entire plate of sea-salt cookies.

But the whale *still* looked sad.

"I think she misses her home," Oona whispered to Otto.
The young whale began to wail.

Oona and Otto agreed. Somehow, they'd find her family.

Like most treasure hunters, Oona had a collection
of old ship maps and broken compasses.

She tinkered. And tapped.
And tweezed, until . . .

TA-DA!

It worked!

After a night of rest, Oona, Otto, and the baby whale set out on their long journey north to cooler waters where belugas made their home.

The travelers passed sailboats and swordfish, freighters and Fantails.

As the temperature dropped, the sea and its creatures became more and more unfamiliar.

Oona lived in the water, but she knew a thing or two about the sky. And this one looked like trouble. Messy trouble. Tricky trouble. *Oh no! Here comes a storm kind of trouble!*

The waves grew as tall as mountains. An angry swell tossed Oona into the air!

The compass! Oona reached for it . . .

. . . but it was too late.

The weary crew took shelter with the king crabs and waited out the storm.

When the Arctic sea finally calmed down, Oona examined the map.

It was badly torn and useless.

How would they ever find their way? Oona shivered. The cold water became strangely still as a **GIANT** iceberg pushed toward them like a ghost ship.

Do they swim to the right or to the left? Oona didn't know. She felt like crying.

But there wasn't time. The *pushy, pushy* iceberg was about to **CRUSH** them!

"Swim right!" she ordered.

Oona dove through the icy waters with renewed confidence. She couldn't follow her map, but she could follow her heart.

Oona hoped she was done with surprises, but the ocean had one more in store for her.

The mermaid's name was Siku, which meant "ice." Her adorable friend was Star.

Otto was **starstruck**.

He flipped.

He yipped.

OOPS! He tripped.

The girls giggled.

Oona explained that she was trying
to return the lost whale to her home.

"I can help!" Siku said enthusiastically.

"Tuugaalik!" She whistled,
and a narwhal appeared. His
horn pointed the way.

When the narwhal could travel no farther, polar bears appeared to offer guidance.

Followed by a walrus.

A few kind strangers.

And a flock of snow geese.

For the first time since their adventure began, the young whale smiled and took the lead.

Siku grinned, "She hears her family."

Oona smiled with relief.

Baby Beluga was home.

Oona lived in the water, but she knew a thing or two about the sky. And this one looked like

MAGIC.

Happy magic.

Found magic.

A *new-friends* kind of magic.